BARROUX

Free

OWLKIDS BOOKS

CLAP

CLAP

CLAP

CLAP

CLAP

CLAP

CLAP

CLAP

CLAP

TOOOT!

BANG!

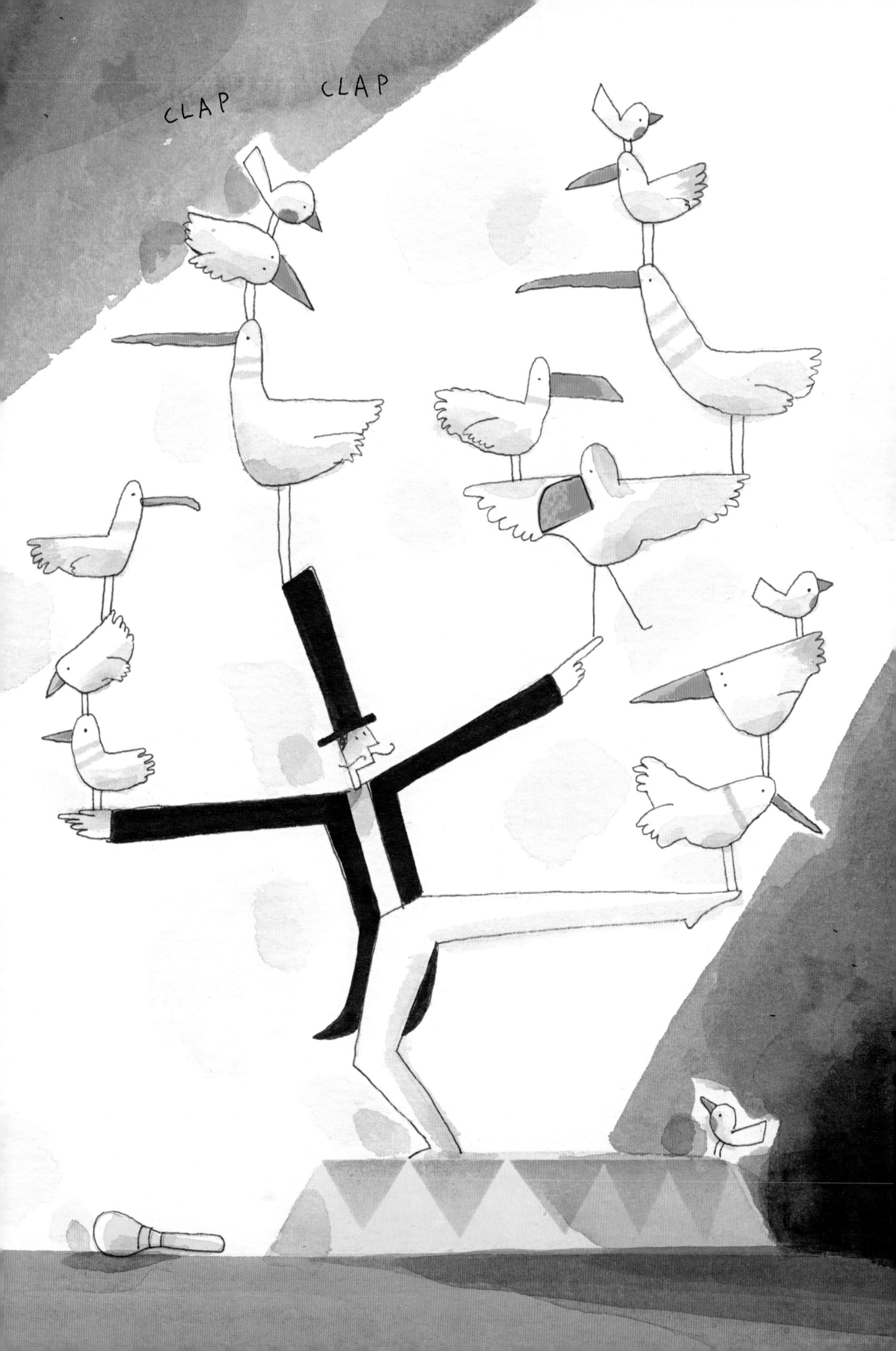
CLAP
CLAP

THE GREAT
BIRD
CIRCUS
CLAP
CLAP
CLAP
CLAP
CLAP

CLAP
CLAP
CLAP
CLAP
CLAP
CLAP
CLAP

Great show, everyone!

Sleep well. Tomorrow is a big day.

TWEEET!
TWEEET!
TWEEET!
TWEET!

We're off to perform for the governor!
It's a very important day for The Great Bird Circus!
TWEEET!
TWEEET!
TWEEET!
TWEEE!
TOOT! TOOT!

TWEEET!
TWEEET!
TOOT!
TOOT!

STOP!

You two can cross.
But for the birds, I need
three copies of form 632BX.
Paperwork from a
veterinarian, including
names of all species and
their nationalities.
Two copies of the R832
certificate for travel in
the Western Hemisphere.
Customs declaration
forms in triplicate.
Border control passports.
Form B780 for the
transportation of wild
birds and animals ...

... and the B612 form
in two copies.

But the governor is
waiting for us.

Not my problem.

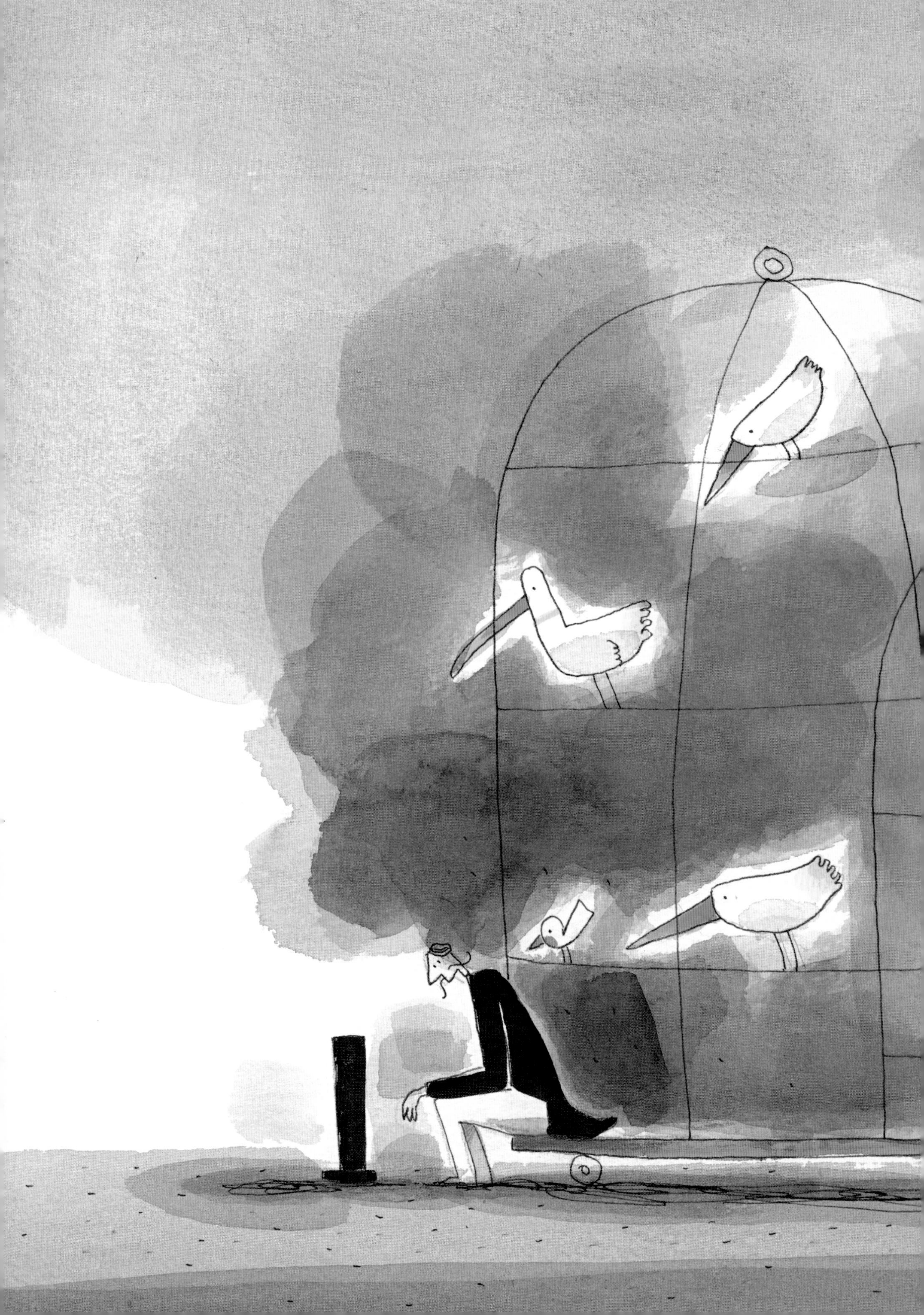

I have an idea!

Fly away, my
friends. You are
free now!

Okay!
Everything
is in order.

You may proceed.

Drive carefully
and have a
nice day!

No
no
Nooo
NOooo
NO

TWEET!
TWEEET!
TWEET!

Welcome back,
my friends.
We missed you.
TWEEET!
TWEEET!
TWEEET!
TWEEET!
TWEEET!
TWEET!

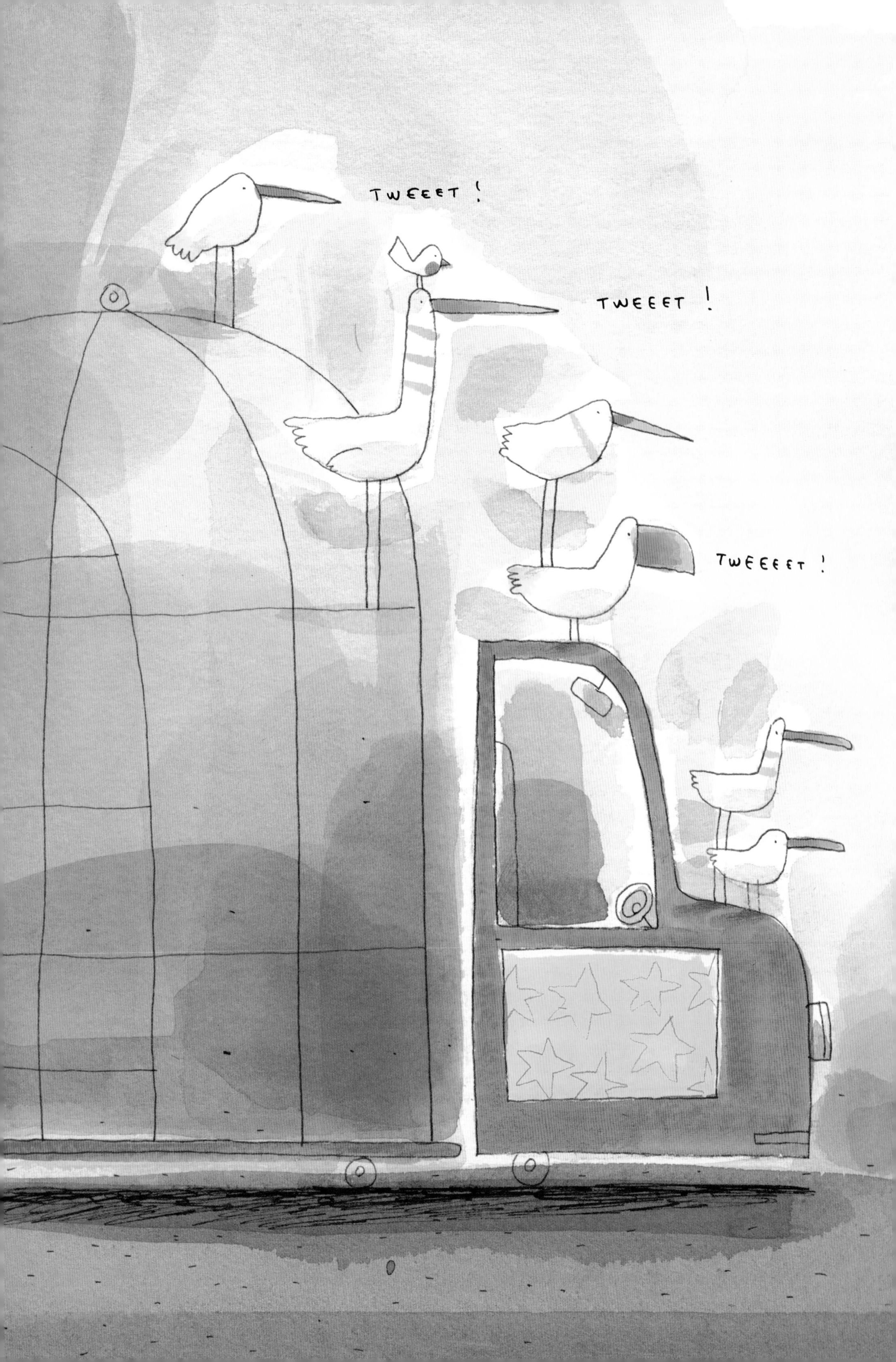
TWEEET!
TWEEET!
TWEEEET!

That was a
good idea, Paloma.
Thank you.

I have
another one! It's
very good!

The End.